THE RESCUE

by Anthony Masters
illustrated by Mike Perkins

Librarian Reviewer
Chris Kreie
Media Specialist, Eden Prairie Schools, MN
M.S. in Information Media, St. Cloud State University, MN

Reading Consultant
Elizabeth Stedem
Educator/Consultant, Colorado Springs, CO
MA in Elementary Education, University of Denver, CO

STONE ARCH BOOKS
Minneapolis   San Diego

First published in the United States in 2008
by Stone Arch Books
151 Good Counsel Drive, P.O. Box 669
Mankato, Minnesota 56002
www.stonearchbooks.com

Originally published in Great Britain in 2002
by A & C Black Publishers Ltd
38 Soho Square, London, W1D 3HB

Library of Congress Cataloging-in-Publication Data
Masters, Anthony, 1940–2003.
   [Freddy's Fox]
   The Rescue / by Anthony Masters; illustrated by Mike Perkins.
   p. cm. — (Graphic Trax)
   Originally published: Freddy's Fox. London: A. & C. Black, 2002.
   ISBN 978-1-4342-0456-1 (library binding)
   ISBN 978-1-4342-0506-3 (paperback)
   1. Graphic novels. I. Perkins, Mike. II. Title.
PN6727.M246R47 2008
741.5'973—dc22   2007030739

Summary: Justin finds an injured fox on his way to school. He wants to help it, but
the bullying Baxter brothers want to hurt it. With help from his best friend, Angie,
Justin hides the wounded animal in the one place the bullies won't go — an old
haunted barn.

Art Director: Heather Kindseth
Graphic Designer: Brann Garvey
Colorist: Nathan Leuth

1 2 3 4 5 6 13 12 11 10 09 08

Printed in the United States of America

TABLE OF CONTENTS

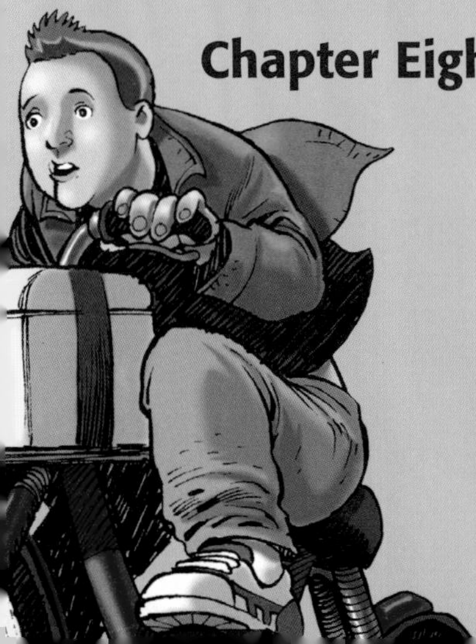

CAST OF CHARACTERS

Justin

Angie

The Baxter Brothers

The Fox

CHAPTER ONE

Bill and Ed Baxter were twins, and the biggest bullies at the school. They were not the kind of people to mess with. Justin was horrified. How could they be so cruel? The brothers even had boys who looked up to them and wanted to be like them.

Everyone looked at Justin in surprise.
No one ever argued with the Baxters.

He didn't care what he said to the Baxter brothers.
He loved animals. Bill turned to Justin.

Ed and Bill were towering over him now.

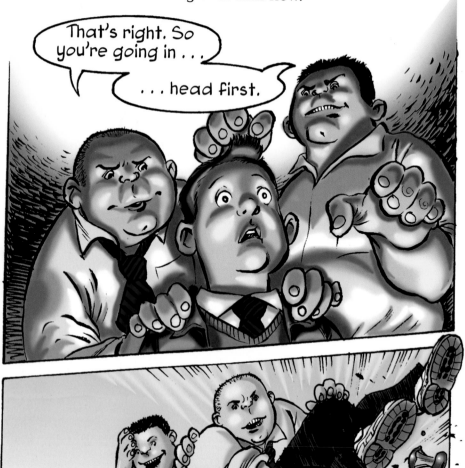

None of the other boys dared to stop them. They just stood watching as the Baxters picked Justin up and dropped him into the barrel. It was full of garbage.

After school, Justin met his friend Angie.

You were in detention today, weren't you?

Yes! Old Mrs. Sanders busted me for not doing my homework.

You haven't heard then.

Heard what?

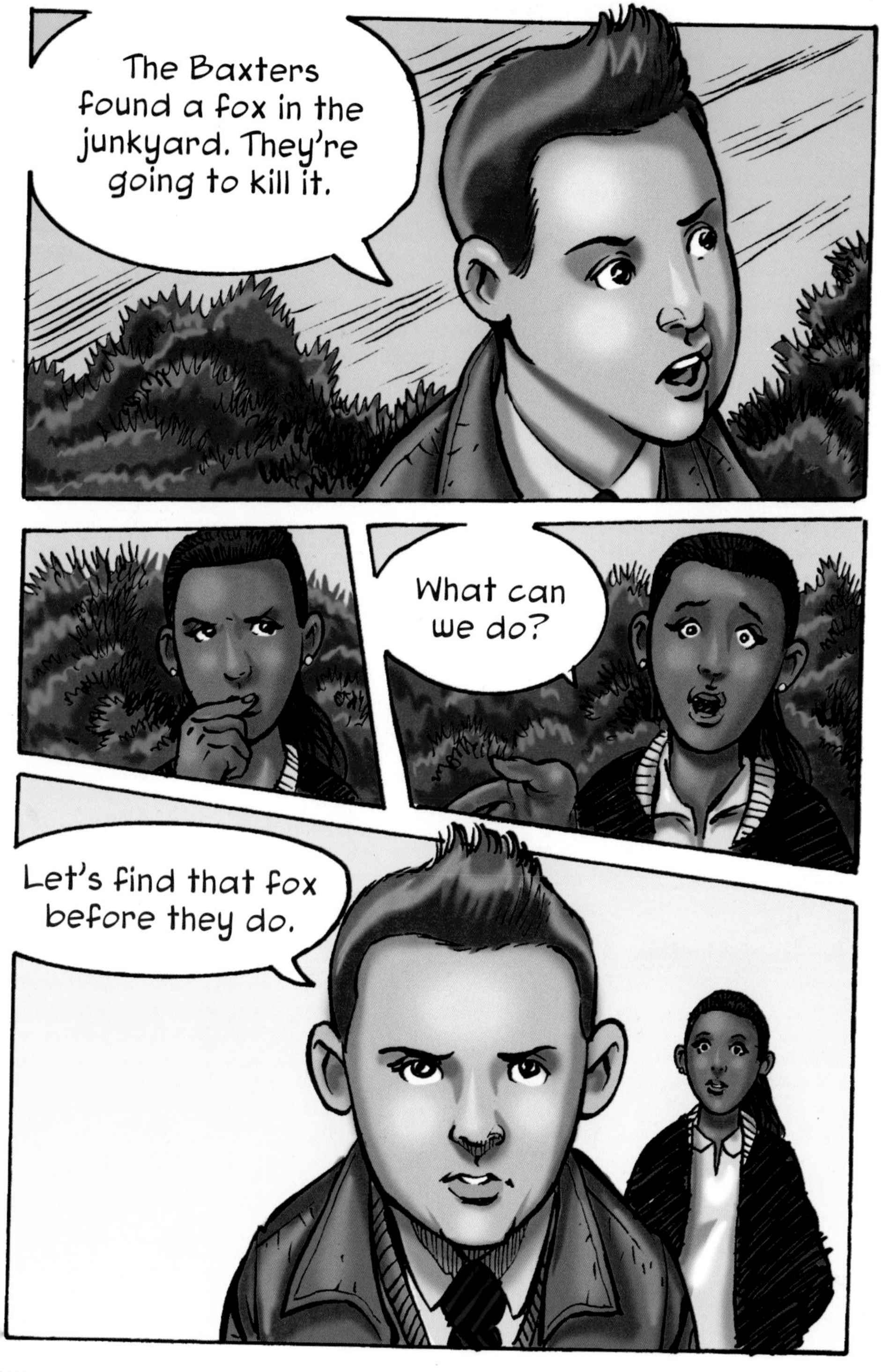
The Baxters found a fox in the junkyard. They're going to kill it.
What can we do?
Let's find that fox before they do.

CHAPTER TWO

Justin and Angie were nervous as they arrived at
the junkyard on the edge of town, but there was
no sign of the Baxters.

In the middle of the yard stood the crushing machine
and a huge crane. There were piles of old cars on one
side of the machine and flattened cars on the other.

Suddenly, Bill Baxter leaped out from behind one of the piles.

So did Ed.

Run!!

Bill was already running over the piles of junk, cutting off their escape route. Justin looked for another way out.

They started running in the other direction, but the Baxters were faster. The twins grabbed Justin and Angie and pulled them toward a giant tank of water.

Just then, there was a shout from the other side of the junkyard.

The man scared them.

The Baxter brothers ran one way.

Angie and Justin went in the opposite direction.

CHAPTER THREE

The next morning, Justin was walking to school when he saw the fox. It was lying on its side under some bushes. Its paw was cut and bleeding. As Justin crouched down beside it, he saw fear in the animal's eyes.

Don't worry, I'm not going to hurt you.

Justin tried to pet the fox, but it opened its mouth and snarled.

Justin wasn't afraid. He loved animals and wanted to be a vet like his uncle when he grew up. He knew the fox needed his help, so he picked it up. For a moment the fox struggled and then stopped.

The fox was gasping for breath and shaking all over.

With the fox in his arms, Justin began to run home.

Suddenly, Justin stopped. Maybe taking the fox home wasn't a good idea. His parents would probably call animal control and have it taken away. He had to find somewhere else to hide it. Then Justin had an idea.

What about old Mrs. Wither's place?

She'd died more than a year ago, and her house was still empty.

Justin ran down a side street and through some gates that led into a garden.

This place is like a jungle.

Some people said that Mrs. Wither's ghost prowled the garden. Feeling a little scared, Justin stumbled along an overgrown path until he came to the house. The paint was peeling and some of the roof had caved in.

There was a long, low building next to the house.

A door swung open. Justin stopped, shivering. In his arms the fox shivered too. Inside, the stables were dark and musty. Justin pushed open the door of one of the stalls and laid the fox on some straw.

After school, Justin returned with a flashlight and a first aid kit. Justin had also brought some dog food, a bowl, and some water. Justin approached the fox slowly and crouched down beside it.

He gently cleaned and bandaged the fox's paw.

Justin was amazed that the fox
didn't struggle this time.

CHAPTER FOUR

Justin came back the next morning. He was relieved to find that the dog food had been eaten, and the fox was sleeping peacefully.

Justin ran all the way to school, catching up with Angie on the way. He told her about the fox and what he had done.

Come with me and see him after school.

What about the ghost of Mrs. Wither?

What about her?

I heard she walks in the garden without her head.

I didn't see her.

Although Angie was a little creeped out, she still went to the garden with Justin after school.

The fox was lying on the straw. He looked at them fearfully.

Justin took off the bandage and washed the fox's paw again. Angie looked outside.

I just saw something move.

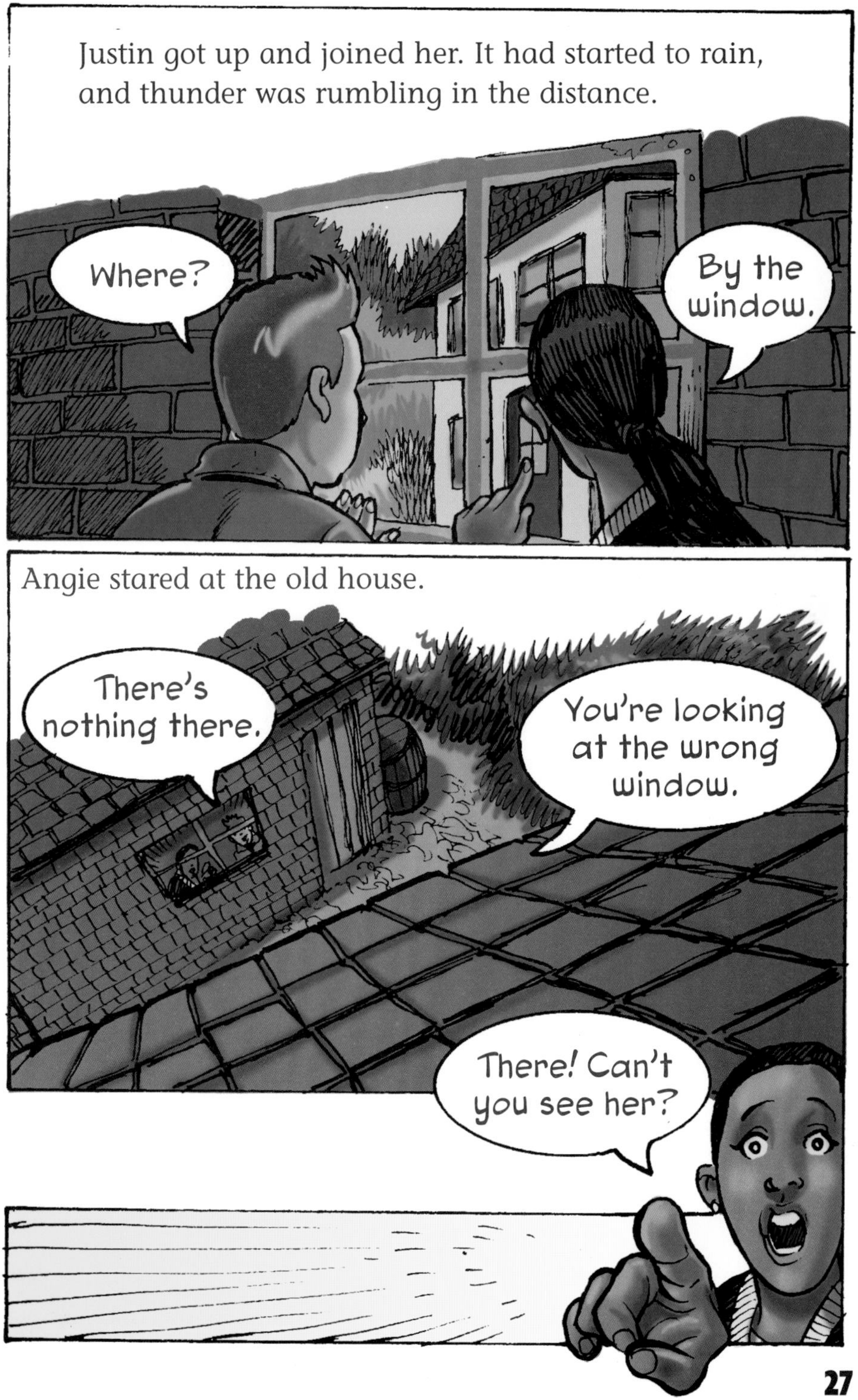
Justin got up and joined her. It had started to rain, and thunder was rumbling in the distance.
Where?
By the window.
Angie stared at the old house.
There's nothing there.
You're looking at the wrong window.
There! Can't you see her?

Angie continued staring at each window. Dark shadows seemed to be moving everywhere.

Angie wasn't in a mood for Justin's joking. Suddenly, lightning flashed in the sky, and Angie began to run.

Justin went back into the stables and knelt down by the fox again.

Justin wasn't sure, but he thought the fox looked a little better. Then the fox licked his hand.

CHAPTER FIVE

The Baxter brothers looked up at their father.

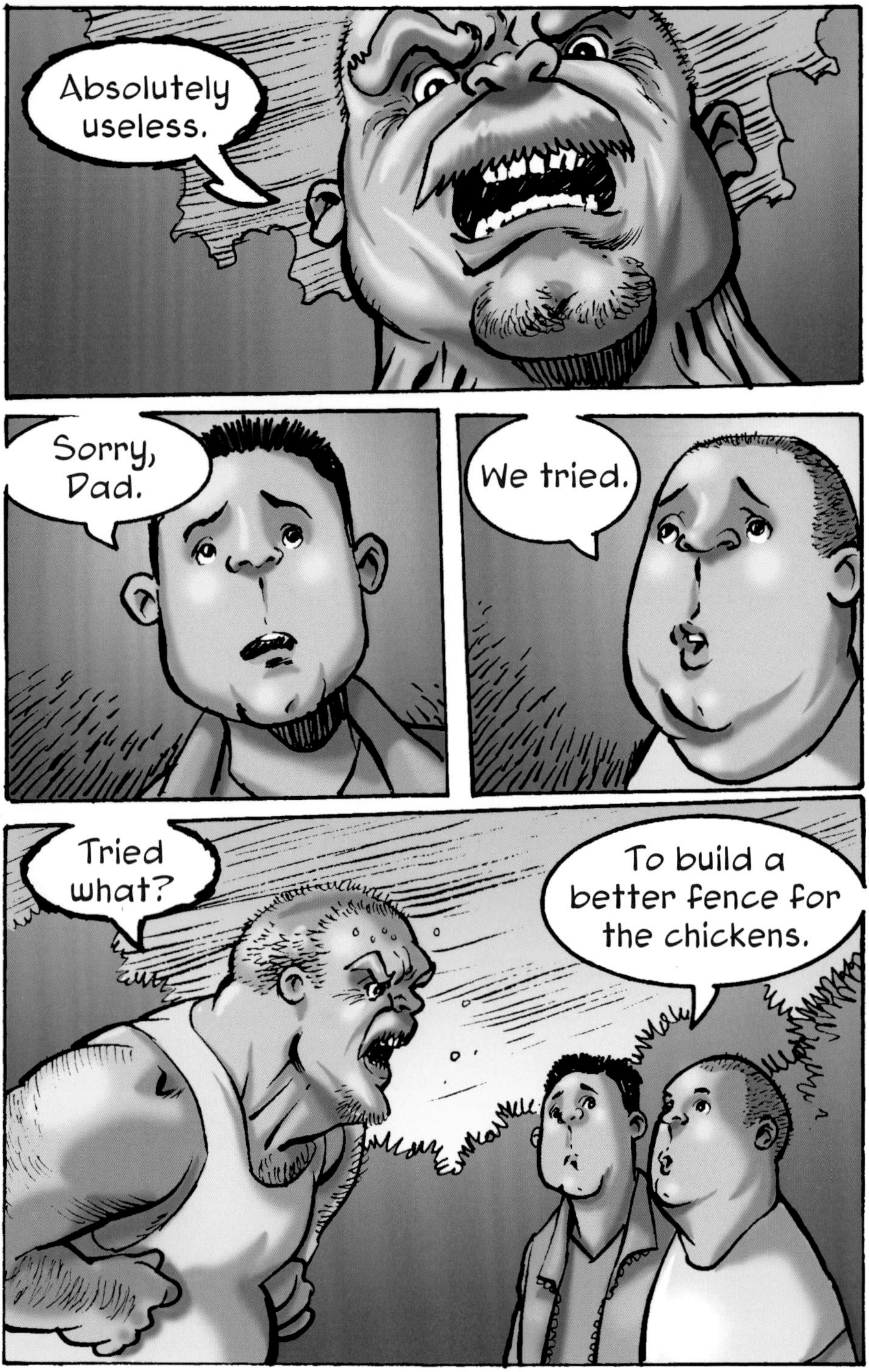
Absolutely useless.
Sorry, Dad.
We tried.
Tried what?
To build a better fence for the chickens.

Ed and Bill said nothing. They were more scared of their father than the chickens were scared of the fox.

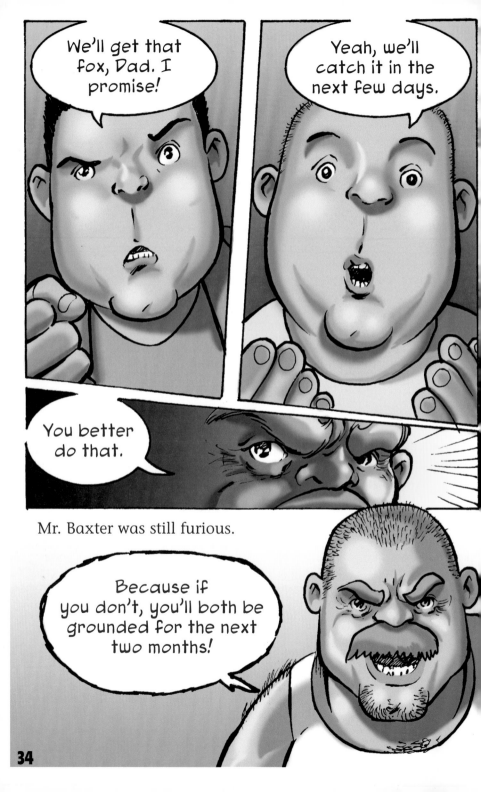

Mr. Baxter was still furious.

CHAPTER SIX

The next morning, Justin was about to head down the path toward the stables when he heard Angie shouting at him. Today was Saturday, and Justin hadn't seen Angie since last night when she ran into the darkness.

They ran into the bushes. As they crouched down, they heard the Baxter twins talking by the gate.

Bill sounded rather nervous.

Their voices faded away, and after a while Justin and Angie got up.

I thought you'd be *too* scared of the headless ghost to come here again.

I'm here.

And I'm staying.

Angie was angry.

When they opened the stable door, the fox was on its feet. It went over to the bowl of dog food and started to eat.

Justin looked down at it.

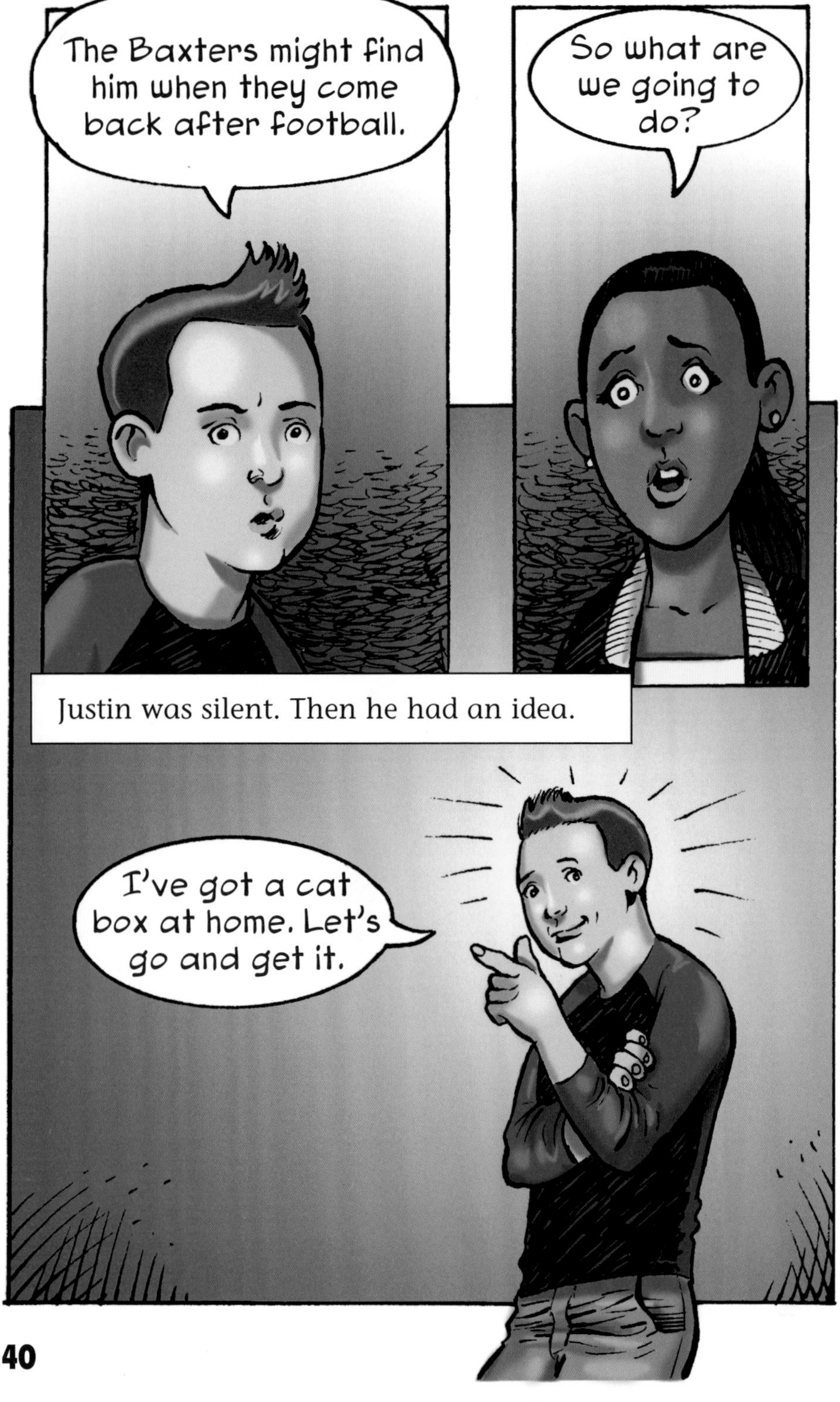
The Baxters might find him when they come back after football.
So what are we going to do?
Justin was silent. Then he had an idea.
I've got a cat box at home. Let's go and get it.

CHAPTER SEVEN

Justin got his bike out of the garage. He found an old strap. Angie helped him attach the cat box to the front of the bike.

Wait a minute, I've got a plan.

Angie ran down the road to her house. Soon, she returned on her own bike with a cat box attached to the front.

Why do we both need a box?

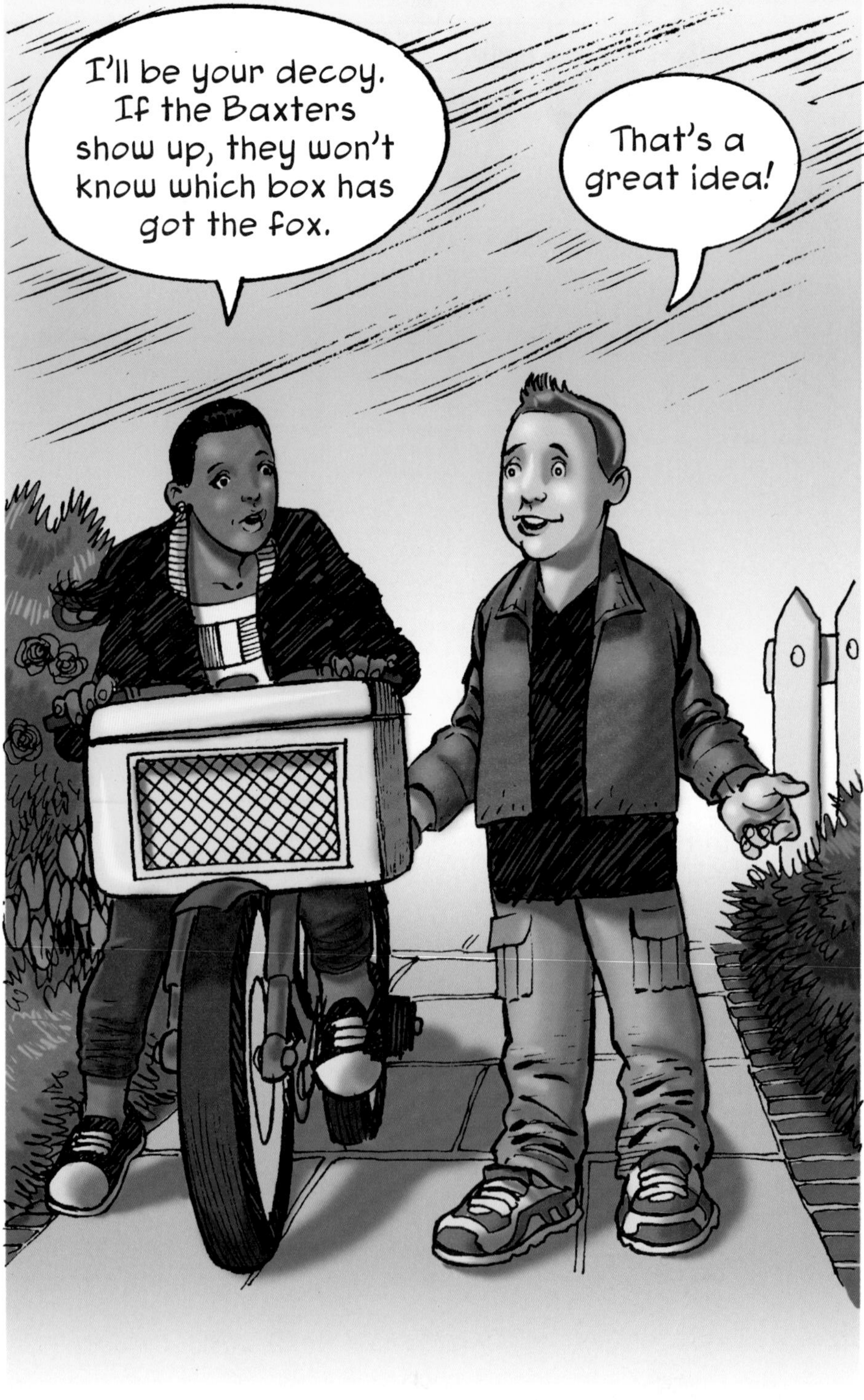
I'll be your decoy. If the Baxters show up, they won't know which box has got the fox.
That's a great idea!

Back at the stable, Justin picked up the fox. It began to struggle.

Eventually, with Angie's help, Justin got the fox into the cat box and shut the lid tightly.

Then he and Angie sped off down the road.
Angie kept looking over her shoulder.

What are you looking for? The ghost?

No. The Baxters. They could be hiding in the bushes, waiting to jump us.

There was no sign of an ambush as Angie and Justin pedaled toward the gates.

I think we're safe now.

Just then they saw the Baxter twins sitting
on their bikes, waiting for them.

Justin sped off and was soon out of sight. Angie pedaled away slowly, so the Baxter twins would follow her and give Justin a chance to get away. It didn't take long for them to pass Angie and skid their bikes across the road to block her.

Ed opened the cat box.

There's nothing inside.

They tricked us!

Justin's got that fox!

They turned their bikes around and started chasing after Justin. Now they were angry. The Baxter twins pedaled faster. Angie watched them disappear into the distance. What was she going to do? Then she had another idea.

CHAPTER EIGHT

Justin was headed for the woods. He pedaled as fast as he could, his bike bouncing up and down on the uneven path. When he looked over his shoulder, he saw the Baxters close behind. Ed was in the lead, looking angry.

Justin wondered what the Baxter twins would do if they caught him.

The path led to a stream. A narrow bridge looked like the only way across.

Justin rode onto the old board and it started to wobble.

Several times he thought he was going to fall
over the edge into the water and drown his fox.

Somehow he got across the board. He pedaled as hard as
he could down the path, heading deeper into the woods.

Then he looked back.

The Baxters were wading across the stream, their bikes over their shoulders. They weren't going to trust the bridge.

I've got to release the fox!

Justin skidded to a halt and leaned his bike against a tree. He knew he only had seconds before the Baxter twins would catch up with him.

Justin opened the cat box and grabbed the fox. He placed it gently on the ground.

The fox crouched down, looking up at him with puzzled eyes.

Justin took the bandage from its paw.

The fox stared up at Justin, looking puzzled.

Ed and Bill jumped off their bikes, flinging them to the ground.

Justin's fox darted through the trees. Both of the Baxter boys ran after it. Justin knew they didn't have a chance of catching the fox on foot.

He got back on his bike, turned around, and began to pedal hard toward town.

Then Justin heard a wild shout behind him and looked back.

The Baxter brothers had given up chasing the fox. Justin breathed a sigh of relief, but it only lasted a second. Now the twins were coming after him. Justin sped up and rode over the bridge without the slightest wobble.

The Baxters decided to risk riding over the bridge this time. But almost immediately they splashed into the stream.

Slowly the Baxters struggled out. They were soaked and covered in mud. Justin had a head start.

Riding toward Mrs. Wither's as fast as he could, Justin hoped Angie had remembered his instructions.

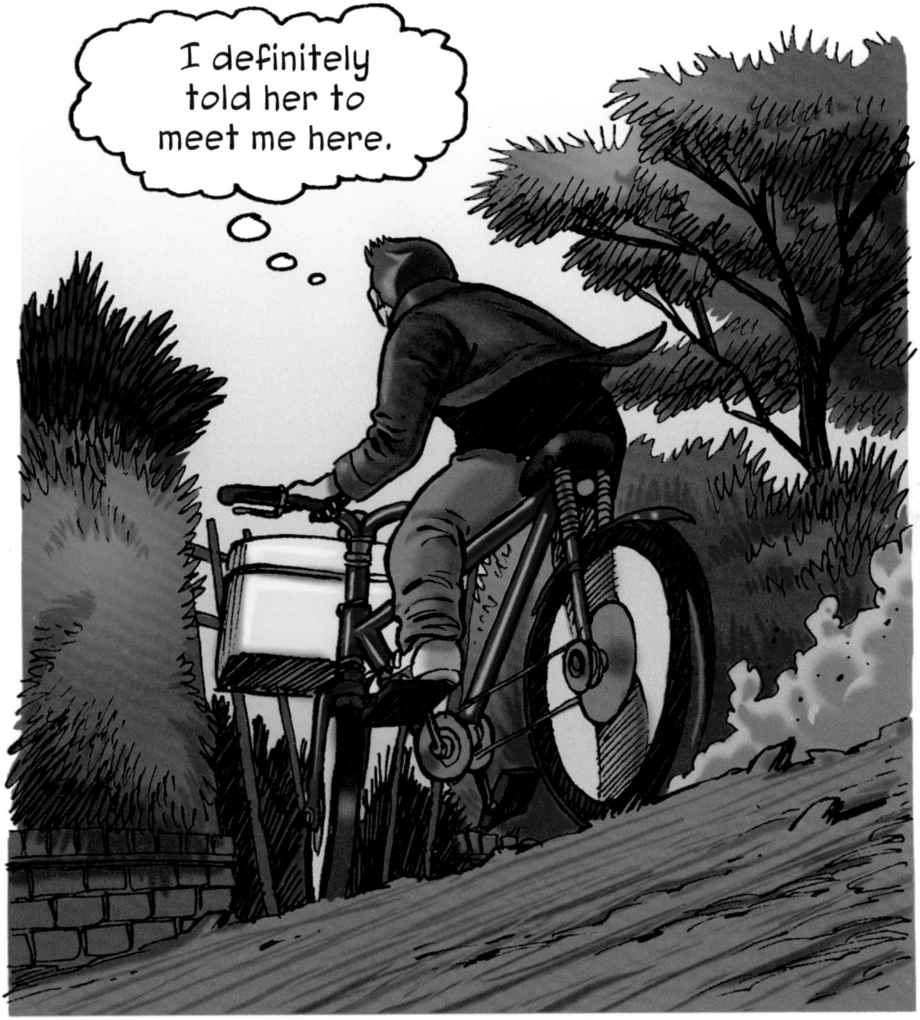
I definitely told her to meet me here.

There was no time to look for her now. The Baxters were close behind again, and Justin knew he had to hide.

He found some thick bushes in front of the
stable. He hid his bike deep inside them,
and then he crawled in too.

Justin was just in time. Peering through the
leaves he could see the Baxters, still soaking
wet and coming down the drive.

As Justin tried not to move a muscle, he heard a strange wailing sound. He glanced up at the sky, shivered with fear, and wondered what the sound could be.

Suddenly, the Baxters started screaming in terror. Justin could hear them pedaling back down the road.

When Justin stood up, he saw a misty figure standing at a second floor window.

Justin looked more closely. He almost screamed as he looked up at the window in terror. The figure was missing something. It was missing a head!

The ghost of Mrs. Wither had come to his rescue.

Justin crouched down under the bush and tried to block out the eerie sound.

He didn't stand up again for a long time.

When Justin finally looked out, he saw Angie running toward him. She had a cloth over her head and a large shaggy mop under her arm. Suddenly, Justin realized what Angie had done for him. She had dressed herself up as the headless ghost of Mrs. Wither.

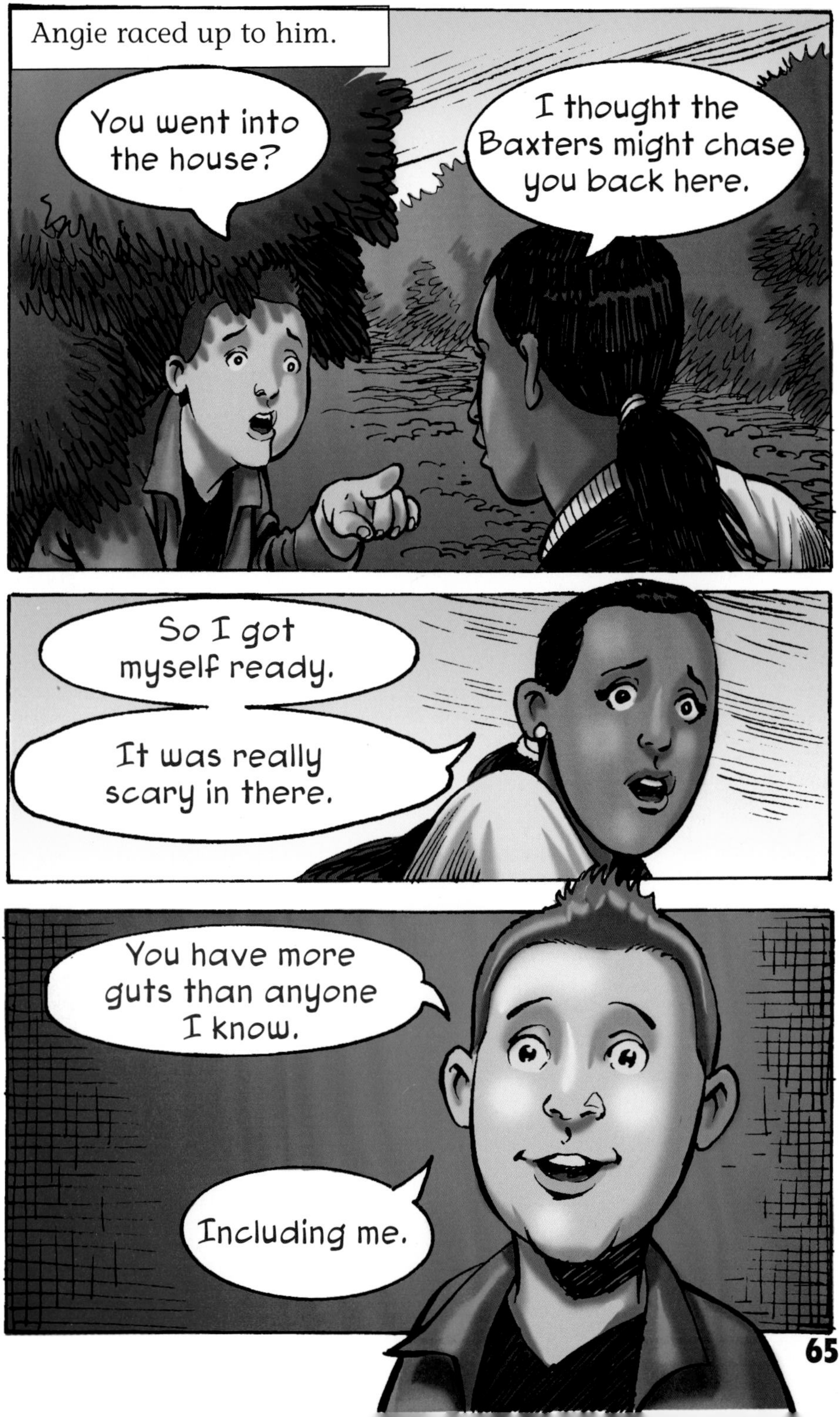
Angie raced up to him.
You went into the house?
I thought the Baxters might chase you back here.
So I got myself ready.
It was really scary in there.
You have more guts than anyone I know.
Including me.

As they rode back home, Justin knew he and Angie would have to keep out of the Baxters' way for a while. But for the moment, they didn't care.

I keep thinking of that fox running free.

So do I. Isn't that great?

ABOUT THE AUTHOR

Anthony Masters published his first book when he was 24. For the rest of his life, he wrote fiction and nonfiction for children and adults, winning awards along the way. *Junior Booklist* magazine once wrote that Masters knew how to "pack a story full of fast-moving incidents." Masters himself once said he would like to be a fox, because the creature is so cunning. Anthony Masters died in 2003.

ABOUT THE ILLUSTRATOR

When he was only eight years old, Mike Perkins started making his own comics and selling them at school during lunchtime. Today, he continues drawing comics, but his art is seen all over the world. As a freelance illustrator, Perkins has worked for companies such as CrossGen, DC Comics, and Dark Horse. He is currently working with Marvel Comics, where he illustrates popular characters like Spider-man, The Fantastic Four, Elektra, and Captain America.

GLOSSARY

ambush (AM-bush)—to attack someone by surprise

animal control (AN-uh-muhl kuhn-TROHL)—a department that handles wild or unwanted animals

decoy (DEE-koi)—someone that draws attention away from another person

detention (di-TEN-shuhn)—a punishment where a student is held after school

furious (FYU-ree-uhss)—extremely upset or angry

horrified (HOR-uh-fyed)—very, very scared

snarled (SNAR-uhld)—showed teeth angrily

stables (STAY-buhlz)—parts of a building where horses or cattle are kept and fed

trespassing (TRESS-pass-ing)—being on someone else's property without permission

vet (VET)—a person who cares for sick or injured animals; **vet** is short for veterinarian.

wailing (WALE-ing)—a loud, crying sound

wobble (WOB-uhl)—to move unsteadily from side to side

INTERNET SITES

Do you want to know more about subjects related to this book? Or are you interested in learning about other topics? Then check out FactHound, a fun, easy way to find Internet sites.

Our investigative staff has already sniffed out great sites for you!

Here's how to use FactHound:

1. Visit *www.facthound.com*

2. Select your grade level.

3. To learn more about subjects related to this book, type in the book's ISBN number: **9781434204561**.

4. Click the **Fetch It** button.

FactHound will fetch the best Internet sites for you.

DISCUSSION QUESTIONS

1. Do you think Justin should have helped the injured fox? Was this decision safe? What would you do if you found an injured wild animal?

2. Justin had to worry about the Baxter twins and the headless ghost. Which of these problems would scare you the most? Explain your answer.

3. Why do you think the Baxter twins are so mean? Explain your answer.

WRITING PROMPTS

1. Animals can make great characters and add action to a story. Write a story using an animal as one of the main characters.

2. Describe a time when someone picked on you or you saw someone being bullied. How did it make you feel? What did you do to stop it?

3. In this story, Mrs. Wither's garden was said to be haunted by a ghost. Write about a place in your neighborhood that is scary or spooky.

ALSO PUBLISHED BY STONE ARCH BOOKS

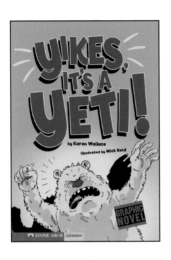